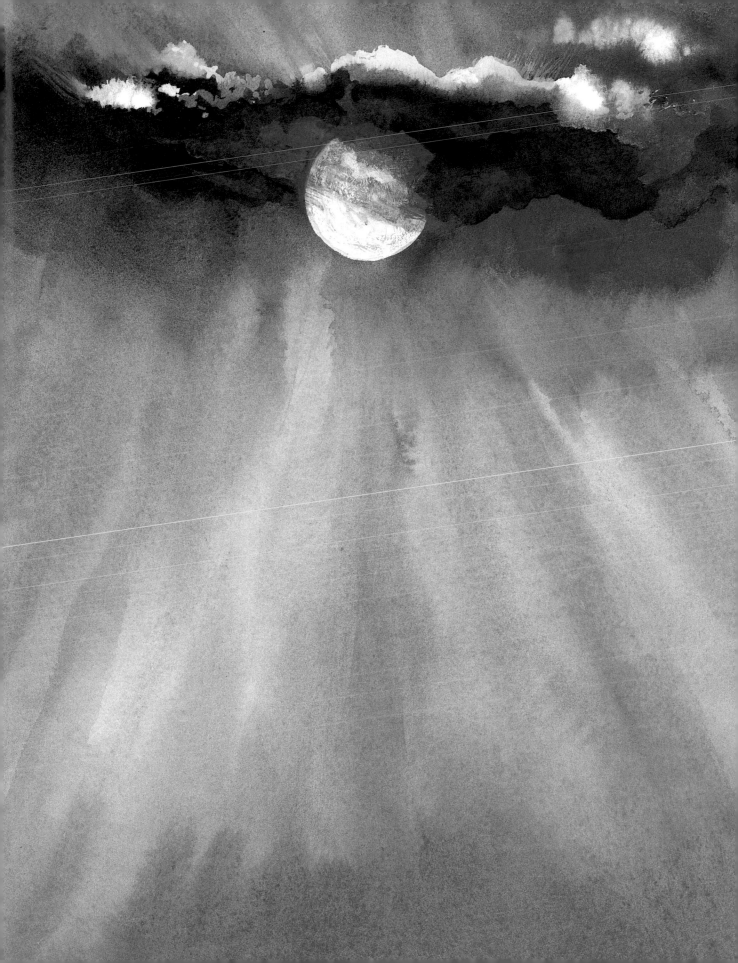

For Tom, with love

DK Publishing, Inc.
95 Madison Avenue
New York, New York 10016

Visit us on the World Wide Web at http://www.dk.com

Library of Congress Cataloging-in-Publication Data
Hughes, Shirley
Abel's moon / Shirley Hughes. -- 1st American ed.
p.   cm
"A DK Ink book."
Summary: In his absence, Abel's children relive his tales of earlier adventures,
make a moon machine out of an old table, and dream of being joined with him through the all-seeing moon.
ISBN 0-7894-4601-4
[1. Father and child--Fiction. 2. Moon--Fiction. 3. Imagination--Fiction.] I. Title
PZ7.H87395Ab   1999 98-53374
[Fic] --dc21   CIP
                                AC

The illustrations for this book were painted in watercolor.
The text of this book is set in 19 point Cochin

Printed and bound in Singapore

First American Edition, 1999
2 4 6 8 10 9 7 5 3 1

Published simultaneously in Great Britain by Random House UK.

Abel's Moon
Shirley Hughes

A DK INK BOOK
DK PUBLISHING INC.

Abel Grable was home at last. Home from his travels, working here and there. Home to the little house where the gate still squeaked and the garden was as untidy as when he left.

Abel's wife, Mabel, and his three children, Adam, Noah, and baby Ben, rushed to the door to greet him. Skipper the dog was half crazy with joy.

Abel was glad to be at home again, cozy by the fire, telling the family about the jungles he had camped in, where monkeys swung through the trees overhead and crocodiles eyed him from muddy swamps.

He told them how he had taken cargoes of supplies by riverboat to remote places where there were no electric lights or street lamps, only the moon to guide the way.

Adam and Noah loved hearing about his adventures.

"Tell us again! Tell us again!" they pleaded.

Abel decided to write his stories down so he wouldn't forget. He found some paper, sat down at the old flap-top table in the spare room, sucked the top of his pen, and began to write.

But the Grables were a noisy family. Abel could hear Mabel singing along to the radio in her workroom, and Adam, Noah, and Skipper playing at being wild animals in the living room below.

He came to the top of the stairs and called out: "Can you boys try to play a little more quietly, please?"

Then Adam and Noah tried to play quietly. But soon they were making as much noise as before.

Now Mabel and baby Ben were
dancing to the beat. Abel put
his head around the door.
   "Could you turn the music
down a bit, please dear?" he asked.
   "Of course, darling," said Mabel.
   But when he was back upstairs,
Abel could still hear muffled
giggles as they chased each
other around the room.

Abel sighed. Then he had a good idea. He folded up his table and carried it downstairs and into the garden. There he settled down to write under the apple tree. This was a splendid place to work. The noises from the house grew faint. There was only the twitter of birds overhead.

Abel wrote and wrote, filling up page after page. He wrote all day and on into the evening, when the daylight faded and the moon rose to guide his pen.

And on the very first page he wrote: "For my three noisy boys, with much love."

The stories were for them.

Soon the time came for Abel to set out again to find work. He packed his bag, putting in his treasured photographs of Mabel and the children.

Then they all hugged and waved good-bye.

After that the children could make as much noise as
they liked. But they missed their dad very much,
especially Adam. Wonderful letters and postcards
arrived from Abel. But Adam found it very hard to
write back. There didn't seem to be much to write about.

They looked at Abel's postcards. And Noah made
Adam read the stories that Abel had written for them
over and over again till he knew them by heart.

The old flap-top table stayed out in the garden where Abel had left it. It turned green with moss, and a jungle of weeds grew up around it, so thick that you could only get to it on hands and knees.

It was a very wild place.

Adam and Noah made their camp there.
Skipper stood guard. Sometimes they were sure
they could hear monkeys leaping from branch
to branch in the tree above, monkeys who even
threw apples down which landed –
plop! – in the grass nearby.

When they had finished camping they turned the table upside down to make a boat. And they paddled it through muddy, crocodile-infested swamps, taking supplies to people miles and miles away upriver with only the moon to guide them.

Then one day, Adam had an even better idea.

He and Noah turned the table the right way up. Adam made a propeller and nailed it to the top.

And Noah painted a beautiful control panel with lots of dials and switches, knobs and levers.

Then the table wasn't an ordinary table any more.
It was a moon machine, on stand-by for take-off.

That night the moon was so bright that it woke
Adam up. It shone in at his window, seeming
much closer than usual.

Adam crept out of bed
and looked down the
garden at his moon
machine. The shadow
of the apple tree moved
on it like magic.

Abel had told him once
that the moon was a
cold place and its
light was reflected
from the sun.

But Adam knew better
than that. He knew that
the moon was shining down
on him, and on Abel, too.
It shone down on all the
people who loved each
other and couldn't always
be together, beaming
down on each and every
one, no matter how far
away they were.

And one night soon, when the moon was
as bright as this, he and Noah (and Skipper
if he behaved himself) might just take off
in the moon machine. And they would give
Abel a wonderful surprise by dropping in
on him, wherever he was.

And then – it wouldn't be long now, surely – when Abel was at home once more, cozy by the fire in their little house where the gate still squeaked, and the moon machine was just an old table again, lying upside down under the apple tree . . .

. . . then, they would tell him all about *their* adventures.
And Abel would listen in amazement and say:
"Tell me again, boys, tell me again . . ."